MOM

in the dictionary between
LAUGHTER and **NOISE**

Library of Congress Control Number: 2020907762
ISBN: 978-0-578-748740 (hardcover)
ISBN: 978-0-578-68323-2 (paperback)
ISBN: 978-0-578-68407-9 (eBook)
First Printing: August 2020

Published by Alpine Mountain Books, LLC
www.AlpineMountainBooks.com
Photographs and Design by ©Jerry and Barbara Jividen,
except where otherwise noted.
Printed in the USA

Dedicated to

my mom,

Ada Shaffer Brickey,

who shaped many lives

and generations of our family

with her selfless acts of love and devotion;

and to my sister, Linda,

for being the inspiration for this story.

I also dedicate this book

to all the moms

(sisters, daughters, cousins)

in my large and fun-loving family.

MOM

in the dictionary between
LAUGHTER and NOISE

Written by Barbara Brickey Jividen
Photographed by Jerry & Barbara Jividen

Published by Alpine Mountain Books, LLC

I lost my **IDENTITY** somewhere.

I might have lost it today,
but it could have been last week.

Maybe I lost it last month,
or even **last year**!

Could it be in the
kitchen?

But **where** in this
all-night deli!

9

Could it be in the cabinets?

Is it in the fridge?

Or in the oven?

Is it with the groceries?

Or is it in the sink?

Could it be in the dishwasher?

Or is it
with the
leftovers?

Could it be in
one of the
laundry hampers?

Could it be under the couch pillows?

Not that I had time to sit,

but I did
pick up an
armload of toys
from underneath
the
cushioned
cracks!

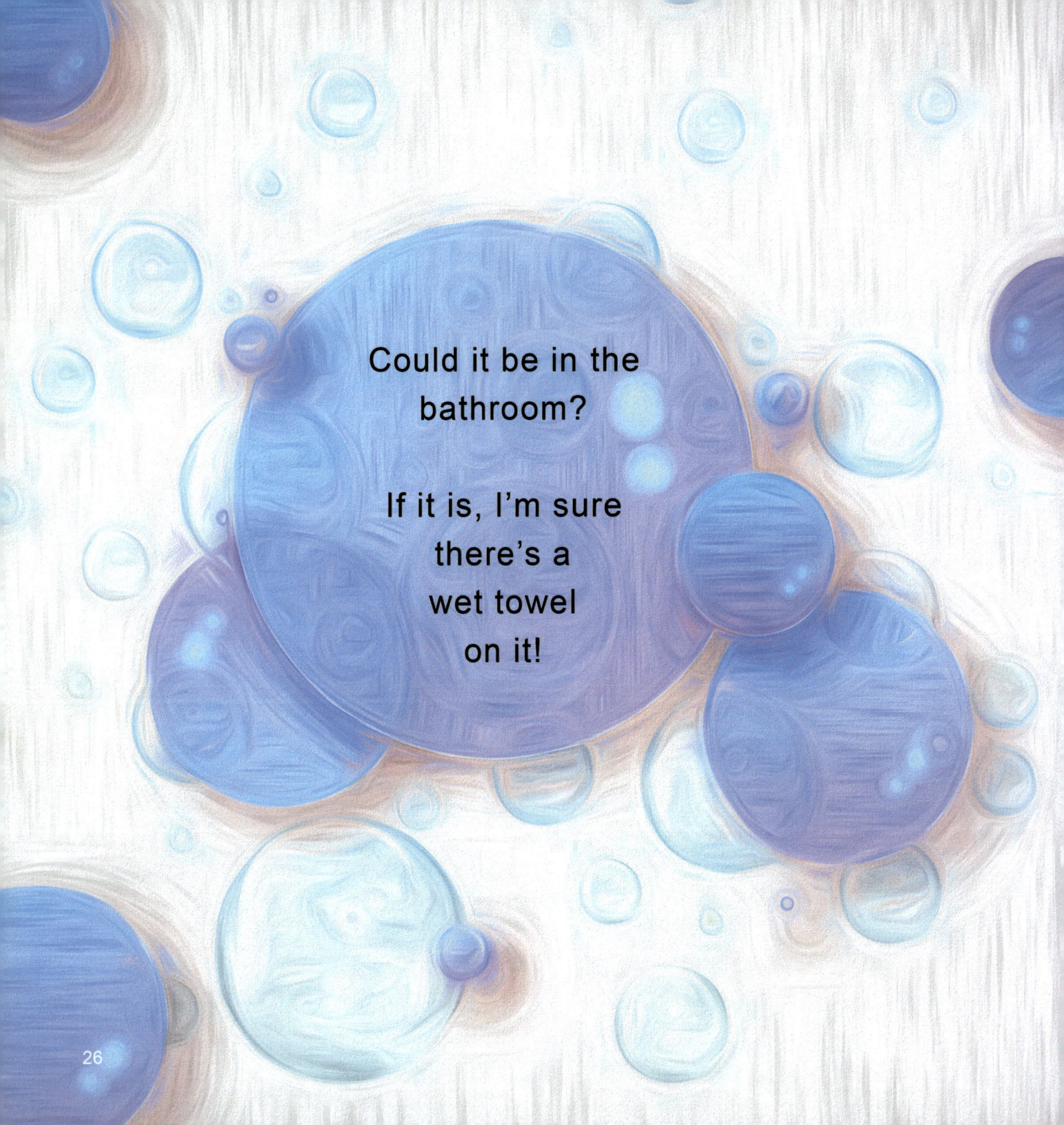

Could it be in the
bathroom?

If it is, I'm sure
there's a
wet towel
on it!

Could it be in the dog house?

Nope...not in there,
but I did find my missing shoe!

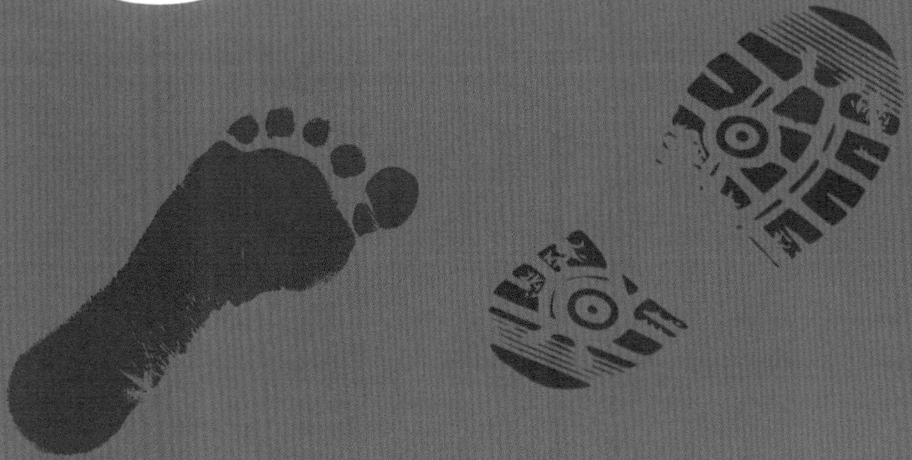

Did I lose it
in the garden
when I was
planting new flowers?

Could it be in the van?

A mother could
lose a kid
in there!

Hmm...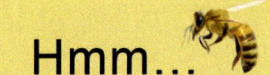

if I could just
retrace my steps,

I'd see that it's **exactly** where I left it!

41

It's
in
a
hug

that barely reaches
around my waist.

It's in the dirty hands
of someone who shares
a mud pie with me.

Abel

It's holding someone
who needs to cry on
my shoulder.

It's with my toddler,
digging for worms!

50

It's in the
thankful hands
that gather
around my
table.

It's in the pride
of my student
with her grade card.

Good job!

Report Card

Scale:
Subject:

	Quarter:				Semester: Year:	
	1	2	3	4	1st 2nd	(Average)
Reading	A	B+				
Language	A	A				
Spelling	A	A				
Writing	A	A+				
Math	B	A				
Science	B	B+				
Social Studies	A	A				
Faith	A+	A+				
Education	A+	A				
	B+	B+				

Grading Scale: A = 90%-100%, B = 80%-89%, C = 70%-79%, D = 60%-69%, F = 0%-59%

Comments:
Amanda is such a kind and courteous student. You should be proud!

It's with the
ball team
eating pizza,

57

not caring
if they
win
or lose!

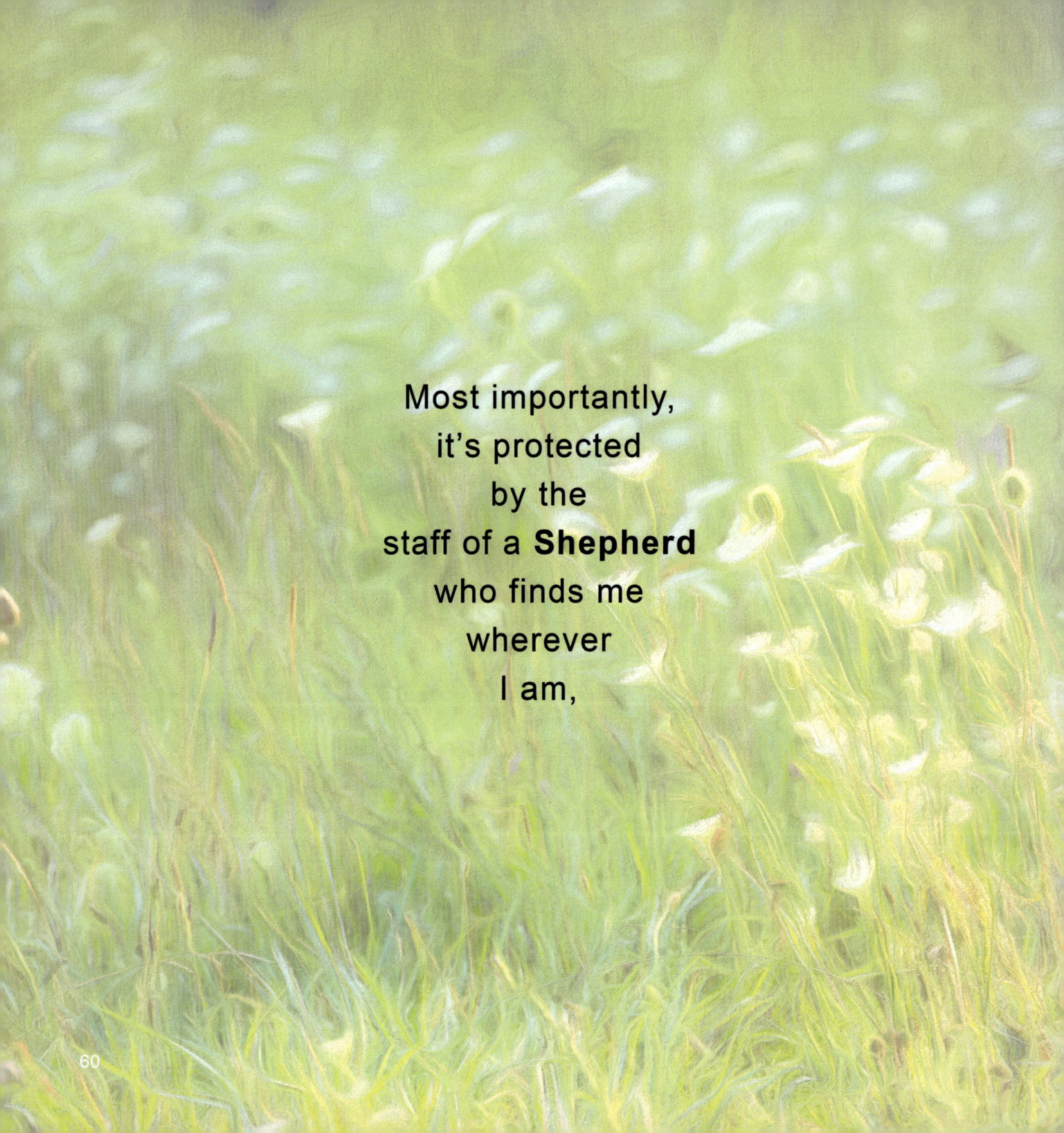

Most importantly,
it's protected
by the
staff of a **Shepherd**
who finds me
wherever
I am,

and
He tells me
that I didn't
lose
my identity...

It's resting

safely

between

LAUGHTER

and

NOISE.

The End

I need a nap!

Thank You!

A very sincere thanks to my cousins,

Elaine & Will, Amanda, Sarah, and "Little" Will Atkins,

who welcomed us into their home

to photograph some of their special moments.

They were the perfect family to model for this book in 2002.

Now, nearly two decades later, their childhood memories and

our family's values can be passed along to future generations

through these pictures and a story that epitomizes mothers everywhere.

Barb & Jerry